BACK TO SCHOOL WITH BETSY

BY CAROLYN HAYWOOD

(available in hard-cover editions)

"B" IS FOR BETSY

TWO AND TWO ARE FOUR

BETSY AND BILLY

PRIMROSE DAY

BACK TO SCHOOL WITH BETSY

HERE'S A PENNY

BETSY AND THE BOYS

PENNY AND PETER

BACK to SCHOOL WITH BETSY

Written and Illustrated
by
CAROLYN HAYWOOD

A Voyager Book
HARCOURT BRACE JOVANOVICH, INC.
NEW YORK

ISBN 0-15-610200-5
Printed in the United States of America
A B C D E F G H I J

To my brother
George

CONTENTS

I. THE OTHER SIDE OF THE GARDEN WALL 3

II. THUMPY AND THE WHITEWASH 23

III. THE WEDDING PRESENT 38

IV. HOW MR. KILPATRICK BLEW HIS WHISTLE 56

V. JIMMY AND CHUMMY 74

VI. THE TALE OF THE BLACKBOARD PICTURE 91

VII. FATHER'S FUNNY DREAM 107

VIII. THE CHRISTMAS SLEIGH RIDE 124

IX. EXACTLY WHAT BETSY WANTED 140

X. THE EASTER CHICK 156

BACK TO SCHOOL WITH BETSY

CHAPTER I

THE OTHER SIDE OF THE GARDEN WALL

IT WAS a warm evening in August. Betsy was sitting on the top of the wall that ran along the back of the garden. Mother's garden was lovely. There were roses and speckled lilies, asters and marigolds. The flower beds had neat borders of tiny fuzzy purple flowers.

Betsy looked down on the other side of the wall. A long time ago there had been a garden there. Long, long before Betsy had learned to climb up and sit on the wall. Now there was just a wild mass of weeds and

CHAPTER I

THE OTHER SIDE OF THE GARDEN WALL

IT WAS a warm evening in August. Betsy was sitting on the top of the wall that ran back of the garden. Mother's garden was lovely. There were roses and spotted lilies, asters and zinnias. The flower-beds had neat borders of tiny fuzzy purple flowers.

Betsy looked down on the other side of the wall. A long time ago there had been a garden there; long, long before Betsy had learned to climb up and sit on the wall. Now there was just a wild mass of weeds and brambles and tall grass. Betsy never climbed over the wall. She didn't like anything on the other side. She didn't like the stone house that stood in the midst of the weeds and the tall grass. No one had lived in the house as long as Betsy could remember.

Sometimes Betsy would walk around the block and look up at the front of the house. It had a big porch that was covered with vines and cobwebs. Some of the windows had been broken and the chimney had fallen down. Betsy thought it was the spookiest house she had ever seen. She never told anyone, but when it was dark she was afraid to pass the house. Betsy didn't know exactly why she was afraid, but the house just made her feel creepy.

As Betsy sat on the wall, she looked across the weeds and tall grass. She could see the back of the house. She didn't know which looked worse, the back of the house or the front of the house.

Just then Betsy's mother came out into the garden. "Why, Betsy!" said Mother. "What are you looking so sober about?"

"I was just thinking," replied Betsy. "Do you suppose that anyone will ever live in that old house, Mother?"

"I wish someone *would* come to live in it," said Mother. "The 'For Sale' sign has been hanging on it as long as we have lived here."

"Maybe if someone lived in it there would be a nice garden," said Betsy.

"Wouldn't that be lovely?" replied Mother. "Then there would be flowers on both sides of the wall."

"Well, I wouldn't want to live in it," said Betsy. "It's too dark and spooky."

"Why, Betsy! How silly of you!" said Mother.

Betsy got down off the wall and began to help Mother pull up some weeds.

"When does school begin, Mother?" asked Betsy.

"In a few weeks," replied Mother.

"I wonder if Miss Grey will be my teacher again?" said Betsy. "I love Miss Grey."

"Oh, Betsy!" cried Mother. "I forgot to tell you. I met Miss Grey on the street the other day. She told me that she's going to be married. She isn't going to teach any more."

Betsy straightened up and looked at Mother. "Miss Grey isn't going to be at school at all, any more?" she asked.

"That's right," replied Mother.

"You mean I won't see her any more at all?" asked Betsy.

Mother looked up from the flower-bed. When she saw Betsy's troubled face, she said, "Why, Betsy darling! Of course you will see Miss Grey again."

"No, I won't," said Betsy, beginning to cry. "I won't see Miss Grey any more if she isn't going to be at school. I won't ever see her."

"Yes, you will, dear," said Mother. "I'll invite her to tea."

"But that won't be like school. In school I saw her every day," said Betsy.

That night when Betsy went to bed she felt very unhappy. She didn't see why Miss Grey had to get married and spoil everything.

The next morning Betsy's friend, Ellen, came to play at Betsy's house. Betsy told Ellen about Miss Grey.

Ellen felt sorry too when she heard that Miss Grey wouldn't be at school.

"I wish we could go to the wedding," said Ellen.

"I don't want to go to any old wedding," said Betsy. "I think Miss Grey is just a meanie to get married."

"I guess you never saw a wedding cake," said Ellen, "or you would want to go. You get a piece in a box to take home."

Just then Billy Porter arrived. Billy was in the same room in school as Betsy and Ellen.

"Hi!" shouted Billy. "What do you know?"

"Plenty," said Betsy. "Miss Grey isn't coming back to school. She's getting married and we'll never see her again."

"Married!" shouted Billy. "What does she want to get married for? She must be crazy!"

"Ellen wants to go to the wedding," said Betsy.

Billy looked at Ellen. "You must be crazy too," he

said. "I'd like to see anybody drag me to a wedding."

"I guess you've never been to a wedding," said Ellen. "You never got any wedding cake to take home in a box."

"What did you say?" asked Billy.

"I said, I guess you never got any wedding cake to take home in a box," replied Ellen.

The children sat quietly thinking. After a while Betsy said, "Maybe we ought to give Miss Grey a wedding present."

"Well," said Billy, "maybe so."

"I think it would be nice," said Ellen.

"You're sure about the cake, aren't you, Ellen?" asked Billy.

"Of course I'm sure," replied Ellen. "I've been to two weddings and I can show you the boxes the cake was in."

"Well, I haven't any money to buy a wedding present," said Billy.

"I haven't any money either," said Ellen.

"And I just spent my last fifty cents for a birthday present for Father," said Betsy.

"We'll all have to earn some money," said Billy.

"Yes," said Betsy. "There is no use deciding on a present until we see how much money we have to spend."

"I can earn some if I deliver orders for Mr. Watson, the grocer," said Billy.

"I can earn some minding Mrs. Plummer's twins," said Ellen.

"Well," said Betsy, "I'll have to find a way to earn some too."

When Billy and Ellen left, Betsy went into the garden. She climbed up on the garden wall. She sat wondering how she could earn some money for Miss Grey's wedding present.

Soon she saw a tall man coming through the weeds and the grass on the other side of the wall. Betsy was so surprised she nearly fell off the wall. She had never seen anyone there before.

The man smiled at Betsy and said, "Hello, there! I am Mr. Jackson. What's your name?"

"My name is Betsy," replied Betsy.

"Well, Betsy, I'm glad to meet you because you are going to be my nearest neighbor. I've just bought this house," said Mr. Jackson, waving his hand toward the old house.

"You have?" said Betsy, in great surprise. "And will there be a garden on the other side of the wall?"

"Yes, indeed," said Mr. Jackson. "Some day there will be a garden but just now I have to fix up the house.

[illegible]
a baby."

"It certainly is," said Betsy.

"And now," said Mr. Jackson, "I'll tell you why I came over to speak to you. Do you happen to have an older brother?"

"No," replied Betsy, "but I have a baby sister."

Mr. Jackson laughed. "I'm afraid your baby sister won't be able to help me out," he said.

"You see," he went on, "there will be workmen in the house and I would like to find a boy who would be willing to go over to the house every day, after the workmen are gone. I want him to make sure that the windows and the back door have been locked. Do you know of any boy around here who would do that? I'd pay him fifty cents a week."

Betsy looked up at the old house that gave her the creeps. "I'm scared of it," she thought. [illegible] Would she have the courage to go up the steps of the old house? She wondered about that.

Mr. Jackson stood waiting for Betsy to answer.

It's a sight."

"It certainly is," said Betsy.

"And now," said Mr. Jackson, "I'll tell you why I came over to speak to you. Do you happen to have an older brother?"

"No," replied Betsy, "but I have a baby sister."

Mr. Jackson laughed. "I'm afraid your baby sister won't be able to help me out," he said.

"You see," he went on, "there will be workmen in the house and I would like to find a boy who would be willing to go over to the house every day, after the workmen are gone. I want him to make sure that the front door and the back door have been locked. Do you know any boy around here who would do that for me? I'll pay him five cents a day."

Betsy looked up at the old house that gave her the creeps. "Five cents a day," she thought. How she would love to make five cents a day! But would she have the courage to go up to the doors of the old house? She wondered about that.

Mr. Jackson stood waiting for Betsy to answer.

After thinking a few moments longer, Betsy said, "Do you think I could do it?"

"Why, of course you could do it," said Mr. Jackson.

"All right," said Betsy. "I'll do it. When do you want me to begin?"

"Tomorrow," said Mr. Jackson. "The workmen leave at five o'clock. You try the doors about quarter past five. And thank you very much indeed. I'll be back next week to pay you."

"You're welcome," said Betsy, as Mr. Jackson walked away.

Betsy scrambled down off the wall and rushed into the house to find Mother.

"Mother! Mother!" she cried. "What do you think! Somebody has bought the old house! His name is Mr. Jackson and there are going to be workmen fixing the house and Mr. Jackson is going to pay me five cents a day for seeing that the workmen leave the front door and the back door locked." Betsy ran out of breath when she got this far.

"Well, that is good news," said Mother.

"And maybe I'll earn enough money to buy Miss Grey's wedding present," said Betsy.

The next day Betsy could hear the hammers and saws of the workmen. She could see men on the roof and a man fixing the chimney. Betsy thought the house looked more cheerful now that the workmen were in it. But at five o'clock, when the workmen left, it looked just as gloomy as ever. Betsy felt that her courage was running right out of her fingers and toes. By quarter past five she wondered how she could ever have enough courage to go over and try the doors.

The thought came to her to ask Mother to do it. "But that wouldn't be earning the five cents," thought Betsy. "And I don't want Mother to think that I'm a fraidie-cat."

Betsy climbed up on the wall. Then she scrambled down the other side. The tall grass came up to her waist. Brambles scratched her bare legs. Soon she reached the old stone path that led to the back of the house. The stones were almost covered with the grass that had grown up between them. Suddenly a little snake wriggled its way across the path. Betsy jumped. She didn't like snakes.

Betsy ran the rest of the way to the house. She ran up the steps that led to the back door. She tried the knob. The door was locked. Then she ran around to the front of the house. She went up the old broken-down steps to the porch. She noticed that the vines had been cut away and the cobwebs were gone. She took hold of the doorknob. The front door was locked too.

Betsy noticed that the windows on each side of the door were clean and new. She peeked through. She could see into the hall. The carpenters had begun to build new stairs. The hall was full of clean new boards. Betsy went to another window. It too had new glass. She looked inside. She guessed this was the living-room. New bricks were piled beside the fireplace. Just then, the rays of the setting sun came through the back window. They filled the room with a golden light.

"Why, it isn't a creepy house at all," thought Betsy. "It's a nice house."

Betsy walked across the porch and down the steps.

As she turned the corner of the house, she saw Mother looking over the garden wall. She waved her hand to Betsy. Betsy waved too. She forgot all about the little snake as she ran along the stone path and through the tangled weeds and grass.

"Mother!" shouted Betsy. "It isn't a creepy house at all! There wasn't anything to be afraid of!"

Mother laughed as she helped Betsy down off the wall. "Is it going to be nice?" asked Mother.

"It's going to be lovely," replied Betsy. "Do you suppose there is a Mrs. Jackson, too?"

"I don't know," said Mother. "We'll have to wait and see."

That night, after Mother heard Betsy say her prayers, Betsy said, "Mother, were you standing at the garden wall all the time?"

"Yes, Betsy," replied Mother, "all the time."

"And were you watching me all the time?" asked Betsy.

"Yes, dear," said Mother, "all the time."

Betsy thought for a moment. Then she said, "That's

just the way God watches me, isn't it?"

Mother leaned over and kissed her little girl. "Yes, my precious, that is just the way God watches you."

CHAPTER II

THUMPY AND THE WHITEWASH

EVERY day at quarter past five Betsy climbed over the garden wall to see if Mr. Jackson's doors were locked. Once she found the front door unlocked, but she knew how to drop the latch and lock it. Betsy wished that she could go in and look all through the house, but she thought it would be more polite to wait until Mr. Jackson invited her.

One evening Mr. Jackson returned. A week had gone by and he had come back to see how the work on the house was coming along. Betsy, Ellen, and Billy were playing in Betsy's garden. When Mr. Jackson saw Betsy, he paid her thirty-five cents and asked her if she would take care of the doors for another week.

Betsy was delighted, for that meant she would have seventy cents by the end of the next week.

Betsy introduced her friends to Mr. Jackson. Mr. Jackson shook hands with Billy and Ellen. Then he said, "How do you think the house looks now, Betsy?"

"I think it looks nice," replied Betsy. "Of course, I've only seen the outside and peeks through the windows."

"Would you like to see the inside?" asked Mr. Jackson.

"Yes, I would," answered Betsy.

"Well, come along, all of you," said Mr. Jackson.

The children climbed over the garden wall and walked beside big, tall Mr. Jackson. Thumpy, Betsy's cocker spaniel, trotted at their heels.

"Is there a Mrs. Jackson, too?" asked Betsy.

"Not yet," replied Mr. Jackson, "but there will be soon. I'm going to be married next month."

"Oh!" said Betsy. "We are all going to a wedding next month. Our teacher is going to be married. I'm going to use the money I am earning to buy her a wedding present. Billy and Ellen and I are going to buy it together."

"Well, that's great!" said Mr. Jackson. "I'm sure it will be a lovely present."

"I wish she wasn't going to get married, though," said Betsy; "because I won't see her any more."

"But Ellen says you get wedding cake to take home in a box," said Billy.

"That's right," said Mr. Jackson.

Mr. Jackson took the children all through the house. Betsy thought it was beautiful. All of the woodwork had been painted and the walls were being covered with pretty paper. Thumpy sniffed here, there, and everywhere.

Mr. Jackson even took them up to the attic. The children thought the attic stairs were wonderful. They didn't know anyone else who could pull attic stairs right out of the ceiling. Their eyes were very wide as they watched Mr. Jackson pull the rope and bring the stairs down to the floor, just like a big ladder. At the same time a trap door opened in the ceiling.

The children climbed up the ladder and went through the trap door. Thumpy scampered up after them. Thumpy thought he smelled a mouse. He sniffed all around the floor, close to the walls. Soon he came upon a little hole in the wall. It smelled very mousy indeed. Thumpy lay down with his nose touching the hole.

"This is the biggest attic I ever saw," said Billy.

"Yes," said Mr. Jackson, "some day we will have rooms up here too."

In a few minutes, Mr. Jackson and the children trooped down the attic stairs.

Mr. Jackson pulled the rope. The attic stairs moved up and the trap door closed.

"You would have a hard time getting out of the attic if anyone ever shut you in, wouldn't you?" said Billy.

"You certainly would," replied Mr. Jackson.

When they got outside, Mr. Jackson made certain that the door was locked. "All locked up tight," he said.

"Thank you for letting us see the house," said Betsy.

"Yes," said Ellen; "it's very pretty."

"They're swell attic stairs," said Billy.

"Glad you like it," said Mr. Jackson. "Wait until you see the future Mrs. Jackson. She's even nicer than the attic stairs."

"Gee, she must be great!" said Billy.

"I say!" said Mr. Jackson. "How would you all like to come to my wedding?"

"Oh! I'd like to very much," said Betsy.

"I love to go to weddings," said Ellen.

"Oh, boy!" said Billy. "More cake! And is there ice cream too?"

"Yes, indeed," said Mr. Jackson.

The children said good-by and ran back to Betsy's garden.

Mr. Jackson gathered up some old wood and piled it up on the porch. He thought it would make good kindling.

Just as he was getting into his automobile, Betsy came running toward him. "Mr. Jackson!" she called. "Mr. Jackson!"

"What's the matter?" said Mr. Jackson.

"Mr. Jackson," said Betsy, "Billy and Ellen and I don't think we can come to your wedding. But thank you for asking us."

"Why not?" asked Mr. Jackson.

"Well, you see," said Betsy, "we only have enough money to buy one wedding present."

"Oh, that's all right," said Mr. Jackson, as he started the car. "After all, you haven't known me as long as you have known your teacher."

Betsy ran back to Ellen and Billy. "It's all right," she called. "Mr. Jackson says we can come to his wedding anyway."

The children decided that by the end of the following week they would have a little more than two dollars, altogether. The next question was to decide upon the present for Miss Grey.

They were all sitting on the garden wall, thinking about Miss Grey's present. Suddenly Betsy thought of Thumpy.

"Where's Thumpy?" she asked.

"I don't know," said Billy. "I haven't seen him."

"He was over in Mr. Jackson's with us," said Ellen.

Betsy got down off the wall. "Here, Thumpy!" she called. "Here, Thumpy!" Thumpy didn't appear.

Betsy looked in the house but he was not there. Billy and Ellen called and called but there was no Thumpy.

Betsy began to feel frightened. "Where do you suppose he is?" she said.

The children climbed over the wall and ran back to Mr. Jackson's house. Thumpy was nowhere to be seen.

"Oh, where do you suppose he is?" cried Betsy.

Just then Betsy heard a sharp bark. It sounded far away. She listened. There it was again. "That's Thumpy!" she said. "That's Thumpy's bark."

The children stood very still. There was the sound again. "Where do you suppose he is?" said Ellen.

"Sounds as though he was locked in somewhere," said Billy.

"Oh, Billy!" cried Betsy. "Do you suppose he's locked in Mr. Jackson's house?"

"Betcha I know where he is," said Billy. "Betcha he's locked up in the attic."

"Oh, Billy!" cried Betsy. "Thumpy can't stay in the attic all night. It's getting dark now and he'll howl terribly."

"We'll have to rescue him," said Billy.

"Well, how are we going to rescue him?" asked Ellen.

"Wait till I do some exploring," said Billy. Billy went around the house and tried all of the windows. They were all locked. At last he found a little cellar window that opened when he pushed it.

"Hi!" he called out. "I can get in this window. Then I can unlock the front door for you girls."

Billy tried to see into the cellar but it was all dark. However, he crawled through the window and began to let himself down very carefully. Suddenly his grasp slipped and he went down, kerplunk! There was a terrific splash. Billy had gone right down into a barrel of whitewash.

"Help!" yelled Billy. "Help!"

The two little girls stuck their heads through the window. There was Billy, up to his shoulders in the barrel of whitewash.

Betsy took one look and ran as fast as she could, crying, "Father! Father! Come quick! Billy's in a barrel of whitewash."

Betsy's father dropped his evening paper. In a few seconds he had covered the ground from his house to Mr. Jackson's cellar window.

"Now don't cry, Billy," said Father. "We'll have you out of that in a minute."

The cellar window was too small for Father to get through but Betsy crawled through it. Father lowered her down beside the barrel. Then Betsy ran up the cellar stairs and through the house to the front door. She opened the front door and Father came into the house. He hurried down the cellar stairs. Then he lifted Billy out of the barrel of whitewash.

By this time Betsy's mother had arrived. She had brought a pair of Betsy's overalls with her and an old towel. While Father and Betsy and Ellen went up to the attic to get Thumpy, Mother took off Billy's clothes. There was a hose in the cellar so she turned the hose on Billy and washed off the whitewash. When he was dry, he put on Betsy's overalls.

"I'm afraid your clothes are ruined," said Mother.

"It's a good thing I had on my old shoes," said Billy.

Just as Betsy and Ellen and Thumpy were coming down the front stairs with Father, the front door opened and in walked Mr. Jackson. "Well," he cried, "I was just driving past and saw the lights. I thought I had better come in and see who the bandits were in my house."

Betsy and Ellen both began to tell Mr. Jackson about Billy and how he fell into the barrel of white-

wash. By this time Mother and Billy had come up from the cellar.

Mr. Jackson laughed. Then he went out on the porch and called to someone in his car. "Come on in and meet the bandits," he cried.

To the children's amazement, who should walk through the door but Miss Grey.

The three children rushed to her. "Miss Grey!" they shouted. "Miss Grey! Miss Grey!"

Miss Grey put her arms around the children. "Goodness gracious!" she said. "I wonder if they will ever learn to call me Mrs. Jackson?"

"They just better," said Mr. Jackson, "for that is who you are going to be."

"Oh, Mr. Jackson!" cried Betsy. "It's the wonderfullest thing that ever happened! Now I'll see Miss Grey every day."

"And now we're only going to one wedding after all," said Billy.

"Yes," said Mr. Jackson, "but you can have two pieces of cake, Billy, and two plates of ice cream."

CHAPTER III

THE WEDDING PRESENT

ONE AFTERNOON Betsy and Ellen and Billy all met at Betsy's house. Billy and Ellen had brought the money they had earned to buy the wedding present for Miss Grey. Each of the children had seventy cents. It was all in nickels and dimes. When they put them together in the center of the table, it looked like quite a pile of money.

"Boy!" said Billy. "That's a lot of money. We can

buy Miss Grey a dandy present with all that money."

Just then Betsy's mother came into the room. When she saw the money, she said: "I think I had better give you two one dollar bills. You might lose some of that change."

"Can I carry the money?" asked Billy.

Betsy and Ellen were not sure whether they wanted Billy to carry the money.

"The man always carries the money," said Billy. "See, I can put it in my pocket. It's safe in my pocket."

"Well, all right," said Betsy.

"Be careful of the ten cents," said Ellen.

Billy poked the two one dollar bills and the ten cents into his coat pocket.

"Have you decided what to buy?" asked Mother.

"Not yet," replied Betsy. "We thought we would look in the store windows first."

"That's a good idea," said Mother as the children started off.

They walked toward that part of the town where the shops were.

"Billy," said Betsy, "did you know that Ellen and I are going to be Miss Grey's flower girls?"

"What do you mean, 'flower girls'?" asked Billy.

"We're going to walk in front of Miss Grey at the wedding and carry baskets of flowers," said Ellen.

"Sounds crazy," said Billy.

"And we're going to wear long pink taffeta dresses," said Betsy.

"Gee! I'm glad I'm not a girl," said Billy, jumping over a fire-plug.

"Billy, you've still got the money, haven't you?" shouted Betsy.

"Sure," said Billy.

"Well, you better look and see," said Betsy.

"Aw, I've got the money," said Billy, pulling it out of his pocket.

Out flew the ten cent piece to the pavement. Before the children could pick it up, it rolled toward an iron grating and fell between the bars. The children rushed to the grating. They went down on their knees and peered through the bars. There lay the ten cent piece, three feet below.

"Now look what you did!" said Betsy.

"It was your fault," said Billy. "If you hadn't made me look to see if I had the money, it wouldn't have fallen out."

"How will we get it up?" said Ellen.

"I could get it up with some chewing-gum on the end of an umbrella," said Billy. "My daddy got a nickel up that way once. I saw him do it."

"Well, where are you going to get the umbrella?" asked Ellen.

"And the chewing-gum?" asked Betsy.

Billy felt in his other pocket and pulled out a penny. "Now, I'll stay here and guard the dime," he said. "Ellen can take the penny and buy the chewing-gum and, Betsy, you run home and get an umbrella."

The two little girls ran off.

"Hey, Ellen!" cried Billy. "Bring the chewing-gum back to me. It's my penny and I'm going to chew the gum. Get spearmint."

"All right," shouted Ellen.

Ellen was back with the chewing-gum first. By the time Betsy arrived with the umbrella, Billy had the gum chewed up.

"Here's the umbrella," said Betsy. "I brought Father's 'cause it's longer."

Billy took the chewing-gum out of his mouth and put it on the end of the umbrella.

"Wait a minute," cried Betsy. "Don't put all of it on the umbrella, 'cause if it falls off we won't have any more chewing-gum."

"O.K.," said Billy.

He took half of the chewing-gum off. Then he poked the umbrella down through the bars. Just as it was about to touch the ten cent piece, the gum fell off.

"See!" said Betsy. "Now aren't you glad you saved some?"

"Yep!" said Billy, as he pulled up the umbrella.

He put the other piece on more carefully. Once more he poked it down.

"Now be careful," said Betsy.

"Hold your breath," said Ellen.

"Oh, leave me alone," said Billy. "You give me the jitters. I'm going to get it up."

Very carefully Billy moved the umbrella nearer and nearer the ten cent piece. At last the umbrella touched it.

"Is it going to stick?" asked Betsy.

"Be quiet, won't you?" said Billy.

Billy lifted the umbrella.

"It's stuck!" shouted Ellen.

The children held their breath as Billy slowly raised the money. Nearer and nearer the grating it came. At last Billy could reach it. He pulled the coin off the chewing-gum and quickly put it in his pocket.

"Now, let's hurry," said Betsy, "or we'll never get the present."

The children hustled along. Betsy carried Father's umbrella. Before long they came to the pet shop. The children always stopped to look in the window of the pet shop. Today there were some Airedale puppies in one window and a monkey in the other.

"Oh, let's buy Miss Grey a puppy!" shouted Ellen.

"Oh, no!" cried Billy. "Let's get her the monkey."

"No!" said Betsy. "What would Miss Grey do with a monkey?"

"She would like a monkey," said Billy. "I know she would."

"But only organ-grinders have monkeys," said Ellen.

"That's not true," cried Billy, "but I would love to be an organ-grinder if I could have a monkey like this one. Let's see how much it is?"

"Now, Billy, we're not going to buy Miss Grey a

PET SHOP

monkey," said Betsy.

Billy pushed the two little girls into the store. A salesman came toward them.

"How much is the monkey?" asked Billy.

"I don't think we are going to buy it," said Ellen.

"The monkey is twenty-five dollars," said the salesman.

Billy's face fell. "I guess we won't buy it," he murmured.

"How much are the puppies?" asked Ellen.

"The puppies are ten dollars each," replied the salesman.

"Guess we won't buy a puppy either," said Ellen.

"Don't you have anything that is cheaper?" asked Billy.

"Well, we have some nice Persian kittens for five dollars," replied the salesman.

"Anything cheaper than that?" asked Billy.

"How would you like to have a nice rabbit?" asked the salesman, as he led the way to a corner of the shop. "The rabbit is only a dollar."

"That's too cheap," said Betsy. "We have two dollars and ten cents."

"I see!" said the salesman. "Is it for yourselves?"

"Oh, no!" cried the children. "It's for a wedding present for our teacher."

"Well, well!" said the salesman. "Now let me see. We have some canary birds for two dollars, but you would need a cage. You haven't a cage, I suppose?"

The children shook their heads. They hadn't any cage.

"How about some goldfish?" said the salesman. "We have some beautiful goldfish." He led the way to a large tank filled with goldfish. "You could give her three goldfish and you could each pick one out," he said.

"Oh, that would be nice," said Betsy.

"How much would that cost?" asked Billy.

"You could have three for one dollar and a half," said the salesman.

"What would we put them in?" asked Ellen.

"I can let you have a nice bowl for sixty cents," he

replied.

"How much would that come to?" asked Billy.

"Two dollars and ten cents," replied the salesman.

The children beamed. They were delighted. Now they could each pick the fish they liked best and the price was just right.

Betsy picked out a bright orange goldfish. Ellen selected a silvery one with a beautiful fan-tail.

The salesman looked at Billy. "Which one do you want?" he said.

"I'll take the one in the bathing suit," replied Billy.

The salesman and the girls laughed. "Which one do you mean?" said Betsy.

"That one with the stripes," said Billy, pointing to a lovely striped fish.

The salesman laughed very hard as he scooped up the striped fish.

When the three little fishes were safely in a cardboard box filled with water, the salesman wrapped up the glass bowl.

"Now be careful you don't drop these things," he

said, as he took the two dollars and ten cents from Billy.

Billy carried the box of fish, Ellen carried the bowl, and Betsy carried Father's umbrella.

When they arrived at Betsy's house, the children unwrapped the bowl and emptied the water and the fish into it. They were delighted with the present. When they showed it to Betsy's mother, she said, "It is a very nice present indeed."

The children wrote their names on a card and tied it around the bowl with a piece of white ribbon.

"Do we take it to the wedding with us?" asked Billy.

"Oh, no!" replied Betsy's mother. "It must be delivered before the wedding."

Just then Betsy spied Mr. Jackson. He was walking around the outside of his house. "There's Mr. Jackson now!" cried Betsy. "He will take it over to Miss Grey's house for us."

Betsy rushed out into the garden. "Mr. Jackson!" she shouted. "Mr. Jackson!"

Mr. Jackson came over to the garden wall. "Mr.

Jackson," said Betsy, "come over and see Miss Grey's wedding present. We just bought it."

Mr. Jackson leaped over the wall. When he went into the house and saw the bowl of goldfish, he said, "Well, isn't that great! We have received a lot of presents but no one else has given us goldfish."

"I guess we were pretty smart to think of goldfish, weren't we?" said Billy.

"You certainly were," replied Mr. Jackson. "Miss Grey will be just as pleased as I am."

"It's your present too, isn't it?" said Ellen. "Because you are marrying Miss Grey."

"That's funny," said Billy. "We told you that we couldn't buy you a present and now you are getting a present after all."

"And we didn't have to spend any more money," said Betsy.

"Well," said Mr. Jackson, as he went out with the bowl, "we will name the goldfish after the three of you —Billy, Betsy, and Ellen."

"Well, I'm the one in the striped bathing suit," shouted Billy.

CHAPTER IV

HOW MR. KILPATRICK BLEW HIS WHISTLE

BETSY and Ellen could hardly wait for the wedding day to arrive. Betsy's mother made Betsy a pink taffeta dress and Ellen's mother made Ellen one just like Betsy's. The little girls had never had long dresses before and they felt very important and grown up in their long full skirts.

Betsy's dress was finished just two days before the

wedding. When Betsy tried it on with her silver slippers, Father said she looked like a fairy. When she put on her pink bonnet that tied under her chin with blue velvet ribbons, Father said she was almost as beautiful as Mother.

"Well, at the wedding," said Betsy, "I guess I'll be just as beautiful as Mother, 'cause I'm not going to wear my hair in braids. Mother's going to brush it all out, fluffy like."

When Betsy took her dress off, Mother laid it on the guest-room bed. "Betsy," said Mother, "will you get a hanger, please, and hang your new dress in the closet?"

"Yes, Mother!" replied Betsy.

Mother went off to put the baby to bed and Betsy went to her own room to get a hanger. When she reached her room, she heard Billy calling to her from the garden. Betsy went to the window.

"Hello, Billy!" she called.

"Hey, Betsy!" shouted Billy. "Come on down and see what I just found."

Without thinking of the hanger, Betsy ran downstairs and out into the garden. Billy was stooping down in the garden path.

"What is it?" said Betsy.

"It's a great big worm," said Billy.

Betsy stooped down to look at the worm. It was big and fat and bright green. There were colored spots, like jewels, all over it.

"Oh," said Betsy, "that will be a beautiful big butterfly some day."

"How do you know?" asked Billy.

"I had one once and kept it in a box and it wove itself inside of a cocoon. Then one day it came out of the cocoon and flew away. It was beautiful."

"Do you think if I kept this one it would do the same thing?" asked Billy.

"I guess it would," replied Betsy.

"Have you a box that I could put it in?" asked Billy.

"I'll go see," said Betsy, running off to the house.

In a few moments she returned with an empty candy box. "You can have this," she said.

With a little twig Billy guided the worm into the box.

Just then Thumpy trotted past the children. He was carrying a bone in his mouth and he was covered with soft earth. "Oh, Thumpy!" cried Betsy. "You've been digging!"

"And he has dug up a bone," said Billy.

Thumpy started off on a run. He was afraid the children might take his bone away from him. He had dug deep for that bone and he didn't mean to lose it now.

But the children were too much interested in the worm to bother about Thumpy and his bone.

"You don't mind if I take this worm home, do you, Betsy?" asked Billy.

"No," replied Betsy, "but I would like to see it when it turns into a butterfly."

"Oh, sure!" said Billy, as he put the lid on the box.

After about a half hour Billy went home. He carried the box very carefully.

Betsy played in the garden until dinner time. When Mother called her, she went upstairs to wash her hands. Suddenly she remembered her lovely dress. She had forgotten to hang it up.

She went to her closet and took out a hanger. Then she went into the guest-room. Betsy took one look at the bed. Then she screamed. "Thumpy! Thumpy!" For there lay Thumpy, sound asleep, in the very middle of Betsy's pink taffeta dress.

Thumpy jumped from the bed and dashed out of the room. To Betsy's horror, there lay the bone, right in the center of her pink skirt. The marks of Thumpy's paws were all over the dress.

"Oh, Mother! Mother!" she screamed. "Mother, come quick!"

Mother came running up the stairs. When she saw

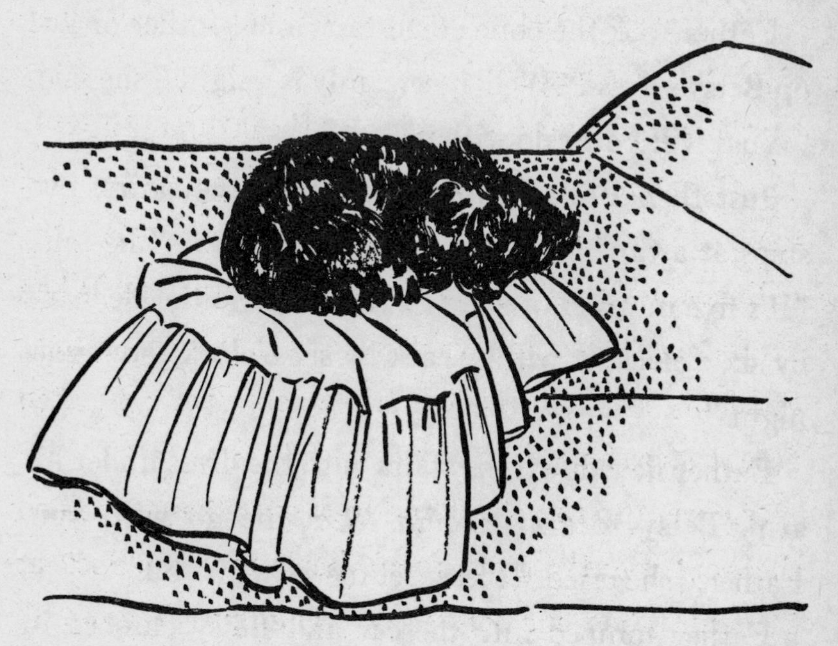

Betsy's dress, she said, "Oh, Betsy! Why didn't you hang it up as I asked you to?"

Betsy began to cry. "I forgot, Mother," she sobbed. "I went out into the garden to see Billy. And now my dress is spoiled and I won't be able to be a flower girl."

By this time Father had arrived. He had come upstairs to see what was the trouble.

Mother picked up the bone and handed it to Father. "Here," she said, "do take this awful bone."

Father took the bone downstairs and Mother picked up Betsy's dress. "Well, it certainly is a sight," she said. "What will I ever do with it?"

Just then Father came dashing up the stairs, two steps at a time. "Give it to me, right away," he said. "It's five minutes of six. If I can get it to the cleaner's by six o'clock, it will be back by six o'clock tomorrow night."

Father flew down the stairs with the dress under his arm. Betsy tore after him. "Let me go with you, Father," she cried. "Please let me go with you."

Father jumped into the car and Betsy climbed in after him.

"I couldn't stand waiting for you to come back," said Betsy, as Father started the car. "I have to see if the cleaner is still open."

Father drove as fast as he could. Soon they were on

the main street. There was a good bit of traffic and Father had to slow down. At the next corner there was a traffic light. Father had to stop. "At this rate we won't make it," he said.

"Oh, Father! We have to make it," said Betsy.

Just then Betsy spied Mr. Kilpatrick, the policeman who always took the children across the street.

When Mr. Kilpatrick saw Betsy, he called out, "Hello, Little Red Ribbons. How are you?"

"Just awful," replied Betsy.

"What's that?" said Mr. Kilpatrick, walking over to the car.

Betsy began to cry again, so Father told Mr. Kilpatrick that they were rushing to the cleaner's with Betsy's flower girl dress.

Mr. Kilpatrick jumped on the running board. He blew his whistle. "Step on it," he said to Betsy's father.

Father stepped on the gas and the car shot ahead. Mr. Kilpatrick kept blowing his whistle and Father drove like the wind, right down the middle of the main street. In no time at all they reached the cleaner's shop.

Mr. Kilpatrick took the dress from Father. Before Father had come to a full stop, Mr. Kilpatrick was at the door of the shop. But the door was locked. The policeman pounded on the door with his great big fist. It made a terrific noise.

In a moment the door was opened. Betsy was on the step now, beside Mr. Kilpatrick.

The storekeeper looked frightened when he saw Mr. Kilpatrick. "What's the matter?" he asked.

"This little girl has to have her dress cleaned by this time tomorrow," said Mr. Kilpatrick, handing over the dress. "It's for a wedding."

"All right," said the cleaner. "I'll see that it is ready for her."

"Oh, thank you, Mr. Kilpatrick," said Betsy.

"That's all right," replied Mr. Kilpatrick. "We can't have Miss Grey's wedding spoiled."

When Betsy finally sat down to eat her dinner, she said, "Oh, Mother, I don't believe I will ever forget to hang up a dress again."

"I certainly hope not," said Mother.

"I hope Thumpy has learned not to get on the beds," said Father.

"Well, I gave him something that should help him to remember," said Mother.

When Betsy's dress came back from the cleaner's, it looked as good as new.

The next day was the wedding. Betsy could hardly wait until the time came to get dressed. She kept looking at the clock and the hands of the clock seemed to move more slowly than ever before. At last the time came. When she was all ready, Father drove Betsy and Mother to the church.

When Betsy saw Miss Grey, she thought she had never seen anyone so beautiful. When Ellen arrived, Betsy said, "Miss Grey looks just like a fairy princess in that white veil."

Betsy and Ellen stood listening to the music of the organ. When they heard the wedding march, they began walking up the aisle.

Betsy could see Billy sitting on an end seat, up front. He was watching them and grinning from ear to ear.

After the wedding was over, the little girls rode back to Miss Grey's house in the big automobile with the bride and groom. Betsy and Ellen had never felt so important in all of their lives.

When they reached the house, they went upstairs to look at the wedding presents. The presents were all spread out on a big table. Betsy and Ellen were pleased to see their bowl of goldfish sitting right in the center of the table.

Soon Billy arrived and he came up to look at the presents.

"I think our present is the nicest," he said to Betsy and Ellen.

Before long the house was full of people. They were laughing and chattering. The dining-room table was covered with plates of sandwiches and cakes. The great big wedding cake stood in the center of the table. It was the biggest cake Billy had ever seen. A waiter stood by the table, cutting brick after brick of ice cream. When Billy took his plate of ice cream, he said to the waiter, "Mr. Jackson said I could have two

plates of ice cream."

"Very well," said the waiter. "Will you have them both at once or one at a time?"

Billy thought this over for a moment and then he said, "I guess I'll have one at a time."

"O.K.," said the waiter.

Billy thought it was very funny that everyone stood up and ate. He always sat down at parties. So he and Betsy and Ellen carried their plates into the hall and sat on the stairs.

When Billy was in the midst of eating his second plate of ice cream, he heard a noise upstairs. He put his plate down and ran up the stairs and into the room where the presents were. What did he find but Miss Grey's Persian cat in the center of the table. To Billy's horror, he had upset the fishbowl. Just as the cat was about to snatch up the striped fish, Billy shouted, "Scat! Get out of there!"

The cat jumped to the floor and flew out of the room.

Billy set the bowl up again and put the goldfish back. He got a towel from the bathroom and mopped up the water. Then he put more water in the bowl. When everything was in order again, he went downstairs.

"What was the matter?" asked Betsy and Ellen.

"Oh, boy!" cried Billy. "The cat upset the bowl of goldfish and he almost ate up Billy in the bathing suit."

"Oh!" cried Betsy. "Are the fish all right now?"

"Sure," said Billy. "I rescued 'em."

Just then Mr. Jackson came along. He had three little white boxes tied with white ribbons. He gave one to each of the children. "Here are your boxes of wedding cake," he said. "If you put them under your pillows tonight, you will marry the person you dream about."

The children took their boxes and said, "Thank you."

The next morning Billy came running into Betsy's house. "Hey, that wedding cake didn't work," he cried. "I dreamed about my grandmother all night. Who ever heard of marrying your grandmother?"

"And I dreamed about goldfish," said Betsy. "I'm not going to marry goldfish."

When Ellen arrived, Betsy said, "Ellen, who did you dream about?"

Ellen looked at Billy. Then she looked down at her shoes and said, "I'm not going to tell you. It's a secret."

CHAPTER V

JIMMY AND CHUMMY

WHEN the day came for school to open, Betsy was up bright and early.

She had new brown oxfords to wear. Betsy had worn sandals all summer. As she looked at them now, lying beside her chair, she thought they looked much older than they had looked when she took them off the night before. They were old and brown and curled up like two autumn leaves. As Betsy looked at them and then looked down at her new oxfords, she knew that the summer was over. It was autumn and she was going

back to school to be in the third grade.

On her way to school, Betsy met Billy. Billy was carrying a candy box. "Hi, Betsy!" shouted Billy. "I'm taking the green worm to school. He's inside the cocoon now."

In a few minutes Betsy and Billy met Christopher. Christopher was wearing a great big hat. It was the biggest hat Billy had ever seen. "Gee, Chris!" shouted Billy. "Where did you get the hat?"

"I got it in Mexico," said Christopher. "And you don't call it a hat. It's a sombrero."

"Well, it looks like a hat," said Billy.

As the children came nearer the school, the crowd grew larger. There were Ellen and Sally and Betty Jane and the twins, Richard and Henry.

The twins had a new dog named Chummy. He was a big red setter. Chummy was following the boys to school. They kept telling him to go back home but Chummy wouldn't go. He had followed the twins everywhere all summer and he had never been told to go home before. He couldn't believe that he wasn't wanted.

"Go home, Chummy," Richard would say, chasing the dog back. "Go home." Chummy would run back a little way. But by the time Richard caught up with the other children, Chummy would be right by the twins' heels again.

Then Henry would try to drive Chummy home. It was no use. Chummy was going where the twins went and nobody was going to stop him.

Before long the children reached the big wide street where Mr. Kilpatrick directed the traffic. Mr. Kilpatrick was taking a group of first grade children across the street.

"Hello, Mr. Kilpatrick," the children shouted.

"We're big enough to go across the street by ourselves now, aren't we, Mr. Kilpatrick?" said Billy.

"Don't be so cocky," said Mr. Kilpatrick, "or you'll go a-ridin' off on somebody's bumper."

"We're in the third grade now," said Betsy.

"Well, you've still got plenty to learn," said Mr. Kilpatrick. "So don't get your head swelled up."

When Mr. Kilpatrick saw Christopher's sombrero, he said: "And sure your head must have begun to swell already, if you have to wear a hat as big as that."

"It's a sombrero," said Christopher. "I got it when I went to Mexico with my daddy. And I rode on a donkey too."

"Mr. Kilpatrick," said Richard, "our dog won't go home."

"His name's Chummy," said Henry.

"Well, what do you expect from a dog named Chummy?" said Mr. Kilpatrick.

"What will we do with him?" asked Richard. "We can't take him in school."

"If we take him home, we'll be late," said Henry.

Mr. Kilpatrick looked at Chummy. Then he took off his hat and scratched his head. "Guess I'll have to take him home myself," he said. "Have you a collar on him?"

"Yes," said Henry, "and it has our address and telephone number on it."

Mr. Kilpatrick took a piece of rope out of the pocket

of his car. He tied it to Chummy's collar. Then he boosted the dog into the red police car and tied the end of the rope to the brake. A great crowd of children had collected around the car.

"Now," shouted Mr. Kilpatrick, "skedaddle, all of you."

The children laughed. They all loved Mr. Kilpatrick. He was so gay and jolly.

"Thank you, Mr. Kilpatrick," shouted the twins.

"Sure, you're welcome," said Mr. Kilpatrick. "But if he bites my head off, you'll have to buy me a new one. And make certain the hair's red."

Chummy looked after the children and whined. He had never been treated like this before. He didn't understand it at all.

The children scampered off, running, jumping, and shouting. A block away from the school they came upon Mary Lou and her little brother, Jimmy. Mary Lou was in great trouble. Jimmy was lying flat on the pavement, screaming at the top of his voice.

The children gathered around Jimmy and Mary

Lou.

"What's the matter with him?" asked Betsy.

"He doesn't want to go to kindergarten," said Mary Lou. "Mamma brought him to school yesterday and put his name down for the kindergarten, and now he won't go."

"I wanta go home," wailed Jimmy.

"I can't take you home," said Mary Lou. "I'll be late if I take you home." Mary Lou began to cry too.

"Wanta go home!" shrieked Jimmy at the top of his lungs.

Just then Betsy had an idea. "Mary Lou," she said, "maybe Mr. Kilpatrick would take him home."

"Yes, maybe he would," said Richard. "He's going to take Chummy home and you live right next door to us."

Mary Lou stopped crying. "Come on, Jimmy," she said, "you can go home"

Jimmy stopped crying. He rolled over on his fat little stomach and got up. Mary Lou took hold of his chubby hand and they started back to Mr. Kilpatrick.

All of the children went with them.

"I don't think Mr. Kilpatrick has gone yet," said Henry.

"I hope not," said Mary Lou.

When Mr. Kilpatrick saw the crowd returning, he called, "Now what's the matter with you? School isn't over already, is it?"

"Mr. Kilpatrick," cried Henry, "Mary Lou's little brother won't go to kindergarten. Will you take him home? He lives right next door to us."

"Bless us and save us!" shouted Mr. Kilpatrick in his great big voice. "Will you ever get to school this morning? Or are you going to spend the morning loading up my car?"

"Will you take him, please?" asked Mary Lou.

"Sure, I'll take him," said Mr. Kilpatrick. "But what I think he needs is to have the seat of his pants warmed."

Mr. Kilpatrick opened the door of the car. Chummy let out a pleased yelp. He thought he was going to get out and go with the children.

The policeman pushed the dog over and put Jimmy on the seat beside Chummy.

"Thank you, Mr. Kilpatrick," said Mary Lou. "Will you tell Mamma that Jimmy was naughty and wouldn't go to school?"

"You bet I will," said Mr. Kilpatrick.

The children started off. They had only taken a few steps when Jimmy opened his mouth again. He let out a piercing scream.

The children turned round.

"Now what's the matter with you?" said Mr. Kilpatrick.

"Wanta go to school!" screamed Jimmy. "Wanta go to school! Wanta go to school!"

"Well, make up your mind," said Mr. Kilpatrick. "If you want to go to school, go to school." He opened the car door and lifted Jimmy out. He set him on the pavement. "Now," said the policeman, "do you want to go to school or do you want to go home?"

"Wanta go to school," said Jimmy.

Mary Lou took hold of his hand again and he trotted

off with the crowd of children.

When they reached the school-yard gate, Jimmy stuck out his under lip. He began to cry again. "Wanta go home!" he yelled. "Wanta go home."

"You can't go home now," said Mary Lou.

Jimmy took hold of the iron fence and held tight. "Wanta go home!" he screamed.

Mary Lou tugged as hard as she could, but Jimmy held on to the fence with all of his might.

Suddenly, through the gate, bounded a big red setter. It was Chummy. He was dragging three feet of rope with him. He dashed up to Richard and licked his face.

"Oh, Chummy!" cried Richard and Henry together.

In a moment Mr. Kilpatrick's red car stopped in front of the gate. He jumped out and ran into the school-yard. "Where's that good-for-nothing dog?" he cried.

In a second he had hold of Chummy's rope. "He broke loose while my back was turned," said Mr. Kilpatrick.

On his way back to the car, Mr. Kilpatrick saw

Jimmy. Jimmy was screaming, "Don't wanta go to school!"

Without a word Mr. Kilpatrick reached down and picked up Jimmy. He stuck him under his arm like a

bag of flour. Jimmy kicked his chubby legs and yelled. But it didn't make any difference to Mr. Kilpatrick.

In a moment the red police car had gone and Mr. Kilpatrick, Chummy, and Jimmy were out of sight.

The children breathed a sigh of relief and went into school.

In the afternoon, when school was over, the children came trooping out. There on the school steps sat Jimmy with the big red setter. Jimmy was looking like a little cherub.

When Mary Lou and the twins saw them, they could hardly believe their eyes.

Jimmy looked up at them with a sweet smile. "We comed back," he said. "Wanta go to school."

CHAPTER VI

THE TALE OF THE BLACKBOARD PICTURE

THE BOYS and girls in the third grade felt very grown up now. Their room was on the second floor.

Betsy liked her new teacher right away. Her name was Miss Ross. She didn't look at all like Miss Grey. Miss Ross's hair was almost black and she had very dark brown eyes. When she smiled it made Betsy think of tooth-paste. By the end of the first day Miss Ross had smiled so many times that all of the children liked the new third grade teacher.

Billy was pleased because Miss Ross was delighted with his cocoon. She put the box on a shelf of the book case. "We'll keep it there," she said, "until the butterfly comes out."

Miss Ross told Christopher that she was glad he had worn his sombrero. She said that the third grade was going to study all about Mexico. Christopher felt very important because he had been there.

"I have a lot of Mexican things," said Christopher. "I can bring them all to school."

"That will be lovely," said Miss Ross.

By the end of the week all of the children were excited about Mexico.

They learned that hundreds of years ago, people came from far across the ocean and made their homes in Mexico. They learned that these people came from the country of Spain and that the people in Mexico still speak Spanish.

The children learned some Spanish words and Betsy was very proud when she said the Spanish words for mother and father.

Mother gave Betsy an old lace curtain which Betsy wore over her head. She called it her "mantilla" and felt very Spanish indeed.

Father said that he felt Spanish too. "Fact is," said Father, "I feel so Spanish I think I will get some tamale plants and raise some tamales in our vegetable garden."

Betsy laughed and laughed. "Oh, Father!" she cried. "Tamales don't grow on plants. They're not vegetables. Tamales are made of corn meal. I don't believe you know any Spanish. You're just making it up."

"Is that so?" said Father. "Well, I know that a burro is a donkey and a hacienda is a farm and an iguana is a lizard and a fiesta is a nice long nap."

"No, it isn't," laughed Betsy. "A fiesta is a holiday and it is like a big fair. A siesta is a nap, Father."

Father laughed and said that he guessed he didn't know much Spanish after all.

The children also learned about the Mexican Indians. They learned that the ancestors of the Mexican Indians lived in Mexico before the Spaniards came.

Christopher said that he had seen lots of Indians. He said they worked on the haciendas. And that they made pottery and wove rugs, just the way their ancestors did. Christopher brought a great many postcards to school. They were nearly all pictures of Indians.

Billy said, "Why are there always mountains in the pictures?"

"Because there are so many mountains in Mexico," replied Christopher. "Nearly everywhere you look there are mountains. Some of the mountains are volcanoes."

Betsy didn't know what a volcano was.

"I know," said Billy. "It's a mountain that explodes every once in a while."

After several weeks Billy said he thought it would be nice to make a great big Mexican picture. Miss Ross said that she thought it would be nice too.

"How big?" asked Betsy.

"As big as you wish," replied Miss Ross.

"Can we cover the whole blackboard?" asked Chris-

topher.

"Yes," said Miss Ross, "it can go right across the front of the room."

"Oh, boy!" said Billy. "That will be some picture!"

"Can we all draw it?" asked Ellen.

"Well," replied Miss Ross, "you can all draw Mexican pictures on paper first. Then we will decide which pictures are the best. The ones that are chosen as the best can draw theirs on the blackboard. The big blackboard picture will be made up of the best little pictures."

Betsy could hardly wait to make her picture. She

loved to draw and she hoped that she could draw on the blackboard. Miss Ross had beautiful colored chalks.

Betsy decided that she would draw an Indian riding on a burro.

Christopher drew a little boy like himself, in a big

sombrero with a blanket over his shoulder.

Many of the children drew Mexican Indians. Some were making pottery. Others were grinding corn and making tortillas which the children had learned are a kind of bread.

Billy made a picture of a Mexican lady seated on a balcony. She was wearing a mantilla.

When the children saw Billy's picture, they were sure that Billy's would be chosen for the blackboard.

Ellen's was nice too. She drew a little Indian girl with a tray full of flowers.

When all of the drawings were finished, Miss Ross hung them across the front of the room. The four best pictures were to be chosen for the blackboard. The children chose Billy's and Betsy's and Christopher's and Ellen's.

Richard and Sally and Peter were chosen to put in flowers and trees. Some of the other children were to work on the wall of the house that formed the background. Others were to put in the mountains and sky.

The children worked every day for weeks on the big

picture. Betsy spent all of her spare time working on her Indian on the burro. Sometimes she even gave up her recess, because she worked more slowly than the other children.

At last the picture was finished. The children were so proud of it they were ready to burst. All of the teachers in the school came in to see it. The children in the older classes came too. Everyone praised the big picture.

"Can't we ask our fathers and mothers to come see it?" asked Billy.

"I think that would be very nice," said Miss Ross.

"When can they come?" asked Christopher.

"Suppose we ask them to come next Friday," said Miss Ross.

Betsy could hardly wait for Friday to come. She wanted Mother and Father to see the lovely picture and especially her Indian on the burro. It was only Tuesday now. Friday seemed a long way off.

Betsy hurried home to tell Mother.

The next morning the children rushed into school

to look at their Mexican picture again. It was so wonderful to have it all finished. Betsy and Billy came through the door first. When their eyes fell upon the blackboard, they stopped still. The blackboard had been washed clean. There wasn't a trace of the beautiful picture.

The rest of the children pushed past Betsy and Billy. They all stared at the blackboard. No one said a word.

Just then Miss Ross appeared and they all began to talk at once. "Miss Ross, what happened to our picture?" they cried.

"I couldn't believe my eyes when I came in this morning," said Miss Ross. "I have just spoken to Mr. Windrim, the janitor, about it. He tells me that he had a new helper yesterday. He told the helper to wash all of the blackboards. He didn't know about our picture."

Betsy felt so badly she put her head down on her desk and cried. The rest of the third graders were as mad as hornets. Billy was furious. He kicked the table leg so hard he hurt his toe.

"Now there is no use being angry," said Miss Ross.

"And it won't help matters to kick the table leg, Billy."

"But all of our good work is gone," said Ellen.

"Well, we'll do it again," said Christopher. "We'll

show 'em. We'll do it all over again. We still have our little pictures. We can copy them again."

"That's the spirit, Christopher," said Miss Ross. "How many boys and girls want to do it over again?"

All of the children but Betsy raised their hands.

Betsy just cried harder.

"Why, Betsy!" said Miss Ross. "You mustn't feel so badly. This time you will do it more quickly."

"But I haven't my little picture of the Indian on the burro," sobbed Betsy. "Everyone else has their little picture, but Thumpy got hold of mine and tore it up."

"Come here to me," said Miss Ross.

Betsy went up to Miss Ross. Betsy's face was covered with tears. Miss Ross put her arm around Betsy. "Now, Betsy," she said, "how did you get the little picture of the Indian on the burro? Where did it come from?"

"I thought of it," said Betsy.

"Well, nothing has happened to your thinker, has it?" said Miss Ross. "Thumpy hasn't torn up your thinker, has he?"

This made the children laugh because they all knew that Thumpy couldn't tear up Betsy's thinker.

Betsy wiped her eyes and her nose. "No," she said.

"Well then, you're all right," said Miss Ross. "You can think it again."

Betsy felt much better as she took her seat.

That afternoon she made another picture of an Indian on a burro. She was surprised to find that she liked it much better than the first one.

In another week the children had covered the blackboard again. Everyone thought that the new picture was much better than the first one.

When the parents came to see the picture, Betsy's father brought enough ice cream for all of the children. He said he thought they all deserved a great big reward.

"Boy, oh, boy!" said Billy, as he dug into a large plate of ice cream. "Am I glad the first picture was rubbed off!"

CHAPTER VII

FATHER'S FUNNY DREAM

THANKSGIVING was hardly over when the children in the third grade began talking about Christmas. The paper turkeys and pumpkins that they had pasted on the blackboard were taken down.

The children were soon busy drawing what they called Christmas presents. They made them on large sheets of paper with colored crayons. With scissors they cut around the edges of the presents. When they were all finished, there were horns and drums, balls and tops and blocks. Some of the little girls had drawn dolls. A few of the boys had made fire engines and airplanes. Billy drew a great big fireplace on the blackboard. Then the children pasted the presents in front of the fireplace.

Way up high on the blackboard Miss Ross drew the chimney. Then she pasted Santa Claus's sleigh and reindeer up in the sky. The children thought the blackboard very beautiful.

At home Betsy was very busy making her real Christmas presents. She made Ellen a necklace of pink beads. For Billy she made a bean bag. It was made of red flannel, cut to look like an apple. Mother cut out a stem and leaves from a piece of green flannel. Betsy fastened them on the bean bag. She knew that Billy would know that it was supposed to be an apple as soon as he saw it.

A week before Christmas there was a great big snowstorm. The children were delighted. They went sledding on the hill. They built forts and had snowball battles. Betsy and Billy made a snow man in Betsy's garden. They put a face on the back of the snow man's

head, just like the one on the front.

When Father asked Betsy why the snow man had a face on the back of his head, Betsy said, "Because we don't think it would be polite for the snow man to turn his back on Mr. and Mrs. Jackson. So now when Mr. and Mrs. Jackson look out of their windows, they will see the snow man's face too."

That evening, before Betsy went to bed, she sat on Father's lap beside the open fire. "Father," said Betsy, "tell me about when you were a little boy." Betsy loved to hear Father tell about the things he did when he was a little boy.

"Did I ever tell you about the biggest snowstorm I ever saw?" asked Father.

"No, you didn't," said Betsy.

"Well," said Father, "when I was just about as old as you are, I went to spend the Christmas holidays with my Uncle Dan and Aunt Mattie. They lived on a farm way up in the northern part of Michigan. All Christmas Day it was cloudy and Uncle Dan kept saying, 'There'll be snow 'fore the night's over. And plenty of it if I'm a good guesser.'

"Before we went to bed, I helped Uncle Dan close the shutters. I could see snowflakes falling, very softly.

" 'Be covered up good, tomorrow,' said Uncle Dan. 'Probably get some good sleighing.'

"I can remember," said Father, "just how I felt when Uncle Dan said the word sleighing. I tingled all over. I had never been for a sleigh ride. I had always visited the farm in the summer. But I had seen the big sleigh in the barn. Many a time I sat in the sleigh and thought how wonderful it would be to go for a sleigh ride. I had seen the sleigh bells too, hanging on the back of the barn door.

" 'Oh, Uncle Dan,' I cried, 'do you think I'll get to go for a sleigh ride?'

" 'Shouldn't be surprised,' said Uncle Dan.

"That night," Father continued, "I had the funniest dream. I dreamed that I was having a sleigh ride. And who do you think was driving the sleigh?"

"Who?" asked Betsy.

"Why, Santa Claus," said Father.

"Oh, Father!" cried Betsy. "And were there reindeer and did you ride through the sky and over the chimneys?"

"No," said Father, "we rode in a sleigh just like Uncle Dan's. Uncle Dan's horses, Chippie and Rob, were pulling the sleigh. I sat up beside Santa Claus. Part of the time he let me drive. We drove a long way. The road led through the woods. At last we came to a house. It was all lit up. Santa Claus stopped the sleigh and we got out. He tied the horses to a post and put blankets over them. Then he took hold of my hand and led me up the steps of the house. It looked like an old inn. Inside, there was a roaring fire in the fireplace. Lying on the hearth were two dogs. When Santa Claus and I went into the room, I heard one dog say to the other, 'How do you feel, Fritzie?'

" 'Hot,' answered Fritzie.

" 'Me too,' said the first dog.

" 'Maybe we better beat it,' said Fritzie.

" 'Maybe we better,' said the first, ' 'fore we turn into hot dogs.' "

"Oh, Father!" Betsy laughed. "The dogs didn't really talk, did they?"

"Yes, they did, in my dream," replied Father.

"So what happened then?" asked Betsy.

"Well, Santa Claus began to laugh and the dogs began to laugh. They laughed and laughed and laughed and then I woke up," said Father.

"And what did you do when you woke up?" asked Betsy.

"I jumped out of bed and ran to the window," said Father. "When I looked out, it looked like fairyland. The ground was covered with a heavy blanket of snow. It hung thick on the trees. And it was still snowing hard."

"Did it snow all day?" asked Betsy.

"All day!" exclaimed Father. "It snowed all day and all night and all the next day. On the second night the wind came up and it howled around the corners of the house and blew the snow into great drifts. By the second day you couldn't see where the roads were and most of the fences were buried. The snow had drifted

against the front of the house so that the front door was covered up. We couldn't open it, the snow was so heavy against it."

"My goodness!" cried Betsy. "How did you get out?"

"We could still use the back door," said Father.

"It finally stopped snowing, late in the afternoon of the second day," he continued.

"And then did you go for a sleigh ride?" asked Betsy.

"Oh, my, no!" said Father. "It was a couple of days before we could shovel a path to the road. First of all we had to shovel our way to the barn so that Uncle Dan could feed the animals.

"By New Year's Day the snow was packed down on the main roads, and every now and then we could hear the jingle of sleigh bells. Every time I heard them, I could feel a tingling right up and down my backbone.

"On New Year's afternoon Uncle Dan said that he would hitch up the sleigh and we would drive over to see Aunt Harriet and Uncle Joe. I went out to the barn and watched Uncle Dan put the harness and the sleigh

bells on the horses. When they were hitched to the sleigh, I could hardly wait to get in. There was straw in the bottom of the sleigh to keep our feet warm.

"Uncle Dan took the sleigh around to the front of the house. Aunt Mattie came out with the rugs. She had a great many and I remember one of them was made of fur. Aunt Mattie tucked the fur rug all around me so that only my head showed. Then we started off. The horses trotted as though they liked pulling the sleigh. How the bells jingled! When we passed other sleighs, everyone shouted, 'Hello!'

"Uncle Dan kept wondering whether we would be able to take the cross country cut to Uncle Joe's. The road lay in the open country. Aunt Mattie said that he had better not try it because we didn't want to get stuck in a snowdrift.

" 'Now, Mattie,' said Uncle Dan, 'there's no cause for you to worry. I can tell where the road is by the fence posts. They're just sticking above the snow.'

"For about fifteen minutes our way lay along the edge of a wood. Then we came to a fork in the road. One road had been traveled. The other looked like icing on a cake.

" 'Here's where we turn,' said Uncle Dan.

" 'Now, Daniel,' said Aunt Mattie, 'you take my advice and take the traveled road.'

" 'Mattie,' said Uncle Dan, 'I know my way. It's perfectly safe.'

"Then Uncle Dan turned the horses into the other road. But the road wasn't where Uncle Dan thought it was. Suddenly, before our very eyes, the horses disappeared from sight. They sank into a snowdrift that covered all but their backbones. The sleigh seemed to be sitting way up high.

"Like a flash Uncle Dan leaped from the front seat onto the back of Rob. He quickly unfastened the harness, and in snow up to his shoulders he led the horses out of the drift. In a few minutes he had them back on the safe road. Aunt Mattie held one of the horses and I held the other. Then Uncle Dan pulled the sleigh around and harnessed the horses again."

"What did Aunt Mattie say?" asked Betsy.

"Aunt Mattie said, 'Daniel, maybe some day you'll learn to take my advice.'

"And Uncle Dan said, 'Maybe so, Mattie. Maybe so. Well, it will make a fine story to tell Harriet and Joe when we get there.'

" 'Humph!' said Aunt Mattie."

When Father finished, Betsy said, "Oh, Father! I should love to go for a sleigh ride!"

"Well, perhaps you can go for a sleigh ride," Father answered. "Perhaps I can hire a sleigh and we can go for a sleigh ride in the big park."

"Oh, that would be wonderful!" cried Betsy. "Do you think we can go soon?"

"I'll see about it," replied Father. "And now you run along to bed."

CHAPTER VIII

THE CHRISTMAS SLEIGH RIDE

A FEW days before Christmas Father said that he had a surprise for Betsy.

Betsy shouted, "I bet I know! It's a sleigh ride!"

"Yes," said Father. "If the snow lasts, I have arranged for a sleighing party. It will be on Christmas Eve. You can invite five of the children from school."

"Oh, Father!" cried Betsy. "It's wonderful! Will we go sleighing in the park?"

"Yes," said Father, "in the park."

Betsy invited Billy and Ellen and Christopher, Mary Lou and Peter. They were just as excited as Betsy was.

Betsy told the children about Father's sleigh ride when he was a little boy. She also told them about Father's funny dream.

"Oh, boy!" said Billy. "I wish I could go sleigh riding with Santa Claus, the way your father did."

When Christmas Eve arrived, the snow was packed hard on the roads. It was so hard and frozen that it was shiny and made a squeaky noise. The night was clear and the stars seemed brighter than ever to Betsy.

By seven o'clock the children were all at Betsy's house. Father put them into the car and drove them to a livery stable near the park. In front of the stable there was a big sleigh with two horses. The sleigh had a high seat for the driver and two wide seats behind that faced each other.

"Now, Billy and Ellen can ride with the driver first," said Father. "Then Christopher and Mary Lou can have a turn, and on the way back Peter and Betsy can ride up front."

This satisfied the children and they scrambled into the sleigh. Father tucked the rugs around them. The

horses stamped their feet and shook their heads. The sleigh bells jingled.

"Are you going to drive the sleigh, Father?" asked Betsy.

"Oh, my, no!" said Father, as he climbed into the back seat beside Betsy. "The driver will be here in a moment."

"I wish we were going for a sleigh ride with Santa Claus, the way you did in your dream," said Billy.

No sooner had Billy said this than the door of the stable opened. Who should walk out but Santa Claus! He was wearing a bright red suit and cap trimmed with fur and he had on high black boots. The sleigh bells around his waist jingled as he walked.

"Hello, boys and girls!" he shouted. "So you're going for a ride with me tonight!"

The children could hardly believe their eyes. They were speechless as Santa Claus climbed up into the driver's seat and took the reins in his hand.

"Gee up!" said Santa Claus to the horses.

The sleigh started with a lurch. They were off!

Billy was the first to find his tongue. He said, "Are you really Santa Claus?"

"Sure, me boy, I'm his twin brother," replied Santa Claus, "and just as good. He'd 'a' come himself but he's having a big night tonight getting up and down chimneys."

"Do you live at the North Pole?" asked Mary Lou.

"Not me!" said Santa Claus. "It's too cold. My whiskers freeze."

"Don't you have to help your brother on Christmas Eve?" asked Christopher.

"No," replied Santa Claus, "I never was any good getting up and down chimneys. Always seemed sort of roundabout to me, but me brother's all for it. Did it even as a little fellow. Never would come in through the door like other folks. It was the chimney for him from the first."

The children laughed very hard and asked a great many questions. They were driving through the park now. It was very quiet. There was no sound but the sound of the sleigh bells. Betsy looked up at the tall trees. The stars peeped between the branches and winked at her. In the distance she could hear other sleigh bells. She burrowed down into the warm rugs and held Father's hand. She felt all happy inside. Betsy hadn't known that a sleigh ride could be so wonderful.

"Let's sing 'Jingle Bells,' " shouted Billy.

They all sang,

"Jingle bells, jingle bells,
Jingle all the way,
Oh, what fun it is to ride
In a one-horse open sleigh."

"Let's sing, 'Two-horse open sleigh,'" said Christopher. "'Cause that is what this sleigh is."

So then they all sang, "Oh, what fun it is to ride in a two-horse open sleigh."

All of a sudden the horses changed their gait. The sleigh jolted and Billy toppled right off the front seat. He went head first into a big snowdrift.

"Whoa!" cried Santa Claus, as he pulled up the horses.

The sleigh stopped and Betsy's father jumped down. He ran back to Billy. The children turned around to see where Billy was. All that they could see were two legs covered with dark green snowpants sticking out of the snowdrift. The legs were kicking furiously.

In a moment Father had pulled Billy out. He looked very much like the snow man in Betsy's garden.

Father brushed him off and they ran back to the

sleigh.

"I fell out," said Billy, when he reached the sleigh.

"You don't mean to tell me!" said Santa Claus. "Sure, and I thought you were practicing diving."

The children changed places in the sleigh. Christopher and Mary Lou sat up with Santa Claus while Billy and Ellen took their seats in the back of the sleigh.

"It's funny," said Christopher to Santa Claus, "but you talk just like Mr. Kilpatrick."

"Yes, you do," cried the rest of the children, "just exactly like Mr. Kilpatrick."

"And who may Mr. Kilpatrick be?" asked Santa Claus.

"Mr. Kilpatrick is the policeman who takes us across the street," said Betsy.

"Oh, that fellow!" shouted Santa Claus. "Sure, I've seen him often. He's got a face like a dish of turnips and hair the color of carrots."

The children laughed. "I don't think it is nice of you to talk about Mr. Kilpatrick that way," said Ellen.

"Sure, there's nobody with a better right," said Santa Claus.

"I think you *are* Mr. Kilpatrick," said Mary Lou.

" 'Kilpatrick'! What a name!" said Santa Claus. "Upon my word, I've killed flies and I've killed mosquitoes and one or two centipedes, but never have I killed any Patrick."

The children shouted with laughter.

By this time the sleigh had reached a house. It stood by the road under tall trees. Lights shone from the windows. It was an old inn.

Santa Claus stopped the sleigh and everyone climbed down. A boy in the yard led the horses to a shed near by. He put blankets over them.

Santa Claus led the way into the inn. There was a fire roaring in the fireplace.

Betsy's eyes were as big as saucers. "Why, Father, it's just like your dream when you were a little boy," she said.

In front of the fireplace there was a table. They all sat down at the table. Santa Claus sat at the head of the table.

"Are we going to have something to eat?" asked Billy.

"We certainly are," said Santa Claus. "What do you want to eat, Billy?"

"Hot dogs," shouted Billy at the top of his voice.

"Yes, hot dogs!" shouted all of the children except Betsy. She was laughing so hard she couldn't say anything. At last she said, "Oh, Father!" and she began laughing again. "Do you remember the hot dogs in your dream?"

Father was laughing too. "Yes," he said, "I remember."

After the children ate their hot dogs and drank big cups of cocoa, they went out to the sleigh. They felt all warmed up.

When they were settled, with Betsy and Peter on the front seat with Santa Claus, they started for home.

"Jingle, jingle, jingle," went the sleigh bells. "Trot, trot, trot," went the horses' feet.

Santa Claus joked with the children all the way back

to the stable. There the children climbed out. They all shook hands with Santa Claus and thanked him for the lovely sleigh ride.

As they got into Father's car, they cried, "Good night, Santa Claus! Good night and Merry Christmas!"

"Merry Christmas!" shouted Santa Claus. "Remember me to Mr. Kilpatrick!"

"Sure!" shouted Billy. "Remember me to your twin brother."

Father dropped the children off, one by one, at their homes.

"Good night!" they each called. "Thank you and a Merry Christmas!"

When Betsy kissed Father good night, she said, "Father, was Santa Claus Mr. Kilpatrick?"

Father laughed. "Well, what do you think?" he said.

CHAPTER IX

EXACTLY WHAT BETSY WANTED

Betsy's baby sister, Star, was a year old. Betsy loved her very dearly. She helped Mother take care of her, and when she played with her it was like playing with a lovely big doll.

One day Betsy was watching Mother give Star a bath. Betsy sat on a little stool. The day before she had been over to visit Mrs. Jackson. Now she was telling Mother all of the news.

"The apartment over the Jacksons' garage is all finished," said Betsy. "It's very nice. Sort of like a big play house."

"Is that so?" said Mother.

"Yes," said Betsy, "and Mrs. Jackson has a new maid coming very soon. She's going to live in the apartment over the garage. Her husband is going to live there too. He's going to be the gardener and drive the car."

"Well, well!" said Mother. "Isn't that fine!"

While Betsy and Mother talked, the baby kept Betsy very busy. She kicked and splashed and played with a rubber duck. Every time she threw the rubber duck out of the tub Betsy picked it up for her. Star thought this was great fun.

"May I shake the talcum powder on her?" asked Betsy.

"Yes," replied Mother as she patted Star dry.

Betsy shook the powder all over the baby. Then she rubbed it with her hand. Betsy thought the baby was the softest, smoothest thing she had ever felt.

"Mother," said Betsy, "do you know what kind of a

baby I want the next time we get one?"

"Goodness!" cried Mother. "You're not thinking of the next baby already, are you?"

"Oh, yes!" said Betsy. "I know exactly what kind I want."

"Well, what kind do you want?" asked Mother.

"I want a little colored baby," said Betsy.

"But, Betsy," said Mother, "we can never have a little colored baby."

"Why not?" asked Betsy. "I saw one the other day.

It was so cunning. It looked as though it was made of a piece of your brown satin dress. Why can't we get a little colored baby?"

"Because, dear, colored babies have to have colored fathers and mothers," replied Mother.

"Well, I know," said Betsy, "but couldn't we get one all ready made? I forget what you call babies that you get all ready made."

"You mean 'adopt' a baby," said Mother.

"Yes," replied Betsy. "Couldn't we 'dopt one?"

"No, dear," said Mother. "Colored babies like to be adopted by colored fathers and mothers."

"How do you know, Mother?" asked Betsy. "I'll bet if a little colored baby could talk, it would say it would like to be 'dopted by us."

"Well now, we won't talk about it any more," said Mother. "You have a dear little baby sister to play with."

"Yes," said Betsy, "but I want a lot of babies. And I like all different colors."

One day during the following week Betsy was coming home from school. When she was a few blocks from home she met a little colored girl. She was about two years old and she was crying. Betsy went up to the

little girl. "What's the matter?" she asked.

The baby just went right on crying.

Betsy looked up and down the street. There was no one in sight. "Where do you live?" she said to the baby. The baby cried harder.

Betsy knelt down beside her. "Are you lost?" she asked.

The baby took hold of Betsy's hand. The baby's hand felt soft and warm.

"Haven't you any mother or father?" asked Betsy.

The baby just sobbed.

The two children were standing in front of a big house. Betsy looked up at the house. Then she led the baby up to the front door. Betsy rang the bell. She waited. In a few moments a lady opened the door. She looked at the two on the step. "Well, what do you want?" she said to Betsy.

"Does this little girl belong to you?" asked Betsy.

"She certainly does not," said the lady. And to Betsy's surprise she slammed the door.

"She's not very polite, is she?" said Betsy to her new little friend.

Tears were still running down the baby's face.

"Don't cry," said Betsy. "There isn't anything to cry about. My mother and father will 'dopt you. It's nice at our house and I'll play with you. I have a baby sister too. And you can play with her."

Betsy and the baby trotted down the street hand in hand. The baby was still whimpering.

When Betsy reached the corner grocery store she went in. She bought two lollipops for a penny.

"Whose little colored baby have you got, Betsy?" asked the grocer.

"I guess she isn't anybody's," said Betsy. "I found her and my mother and father are going to 'dopt her."

"Oh, they are, are they?" said the grocer. "I wouldn't be too sure if I were you."

"Oh, but they will when they see her," said Betsy.

The grocer laughed. "Well, good luck to you," he said.

Betsy gave one of the lollipops to the baby. She put it in her mouth. She was perfectly happy now.

When Betsy reached home they were both sucking lollipops.

"Mother! Mother!" shouted Betsy, as soon as she was inside of the house. "Come see what I found, Mother. Come see!"

"Bring it upstairs, dear," called Mother. "I'm in the sewing-room."

Betsy and the colored baby started up the stairs. It was a little slow because the baby would only put her left foot up.

"What on earth are you bringing?" Mother called.

"It's a surprise," Betsy called back. "Just wait till you see what a nice surprise it is."

At last they reached the top of the stairs. Hand in hand they went into the sewing-room. Betsy's face was beaming. She was so pleased with her new friend.

When Mother saw them she dropped her sewing on the floor.

"Gracious sakes!" she cried. "Where did you get that child?"

"I found her," said Betsy. "She's for us to 'dopt."

"But, Betsy," said Mother, "her mother is probably looking everywhere for her. Where did you find her?"

"I found her on my way home from school," said Betsy. "And I asked her where she lived and she didn't say anything. She just cried awful hard. And I asked her if she didn't have any father or mother and she didn't say anything. She just cried and cried."

"Well, I guess she can't talk yet," said Mother. "I'll have to telephone to the police and tell them that we have found a lost colored child."

"I don't want you to telephone to the police," said Betsy, beginning to cry. "I want to keep her. She's just exactly what I want."

"Now, Betsy darling," said Mother, "you can't have everything you want and you certainly can't have someone else's child."

"Father would let me keep her, I know he would," sobbed Betsy.

"Father would do no such thing," said Mother. "People who steal other people's children get arrested. You don't want to get arrested, do you?"

"But I didn't steal her," sobbed Betsy. "I found her."

"Well, suppose your own little sister, Star, got lost. Wouldn't you want the person who found her to bring her back to us?" asked Mother. "You wouldn't want them to keep her, would you?"

"No," said Betsy, gulping, "I wouldn't."

"Well, this little girl's mother is worried about her," said Mother, as she picked up the telephone.

Betsy sat down on a chair. She took the little colored baby on her lap. The baby went on sucking her lollipop.

Betsy listened to Mother while she gave her name and address to the policeman. Then she heard Mother say, "Do you know of anyone who has lost a little colored girl? She is about two years old."

Betsy could hear the policeman's voice buzzing on the other end of the telephone. She couldn't tell what he was saying.

She heard Mother say, "Why, you don't say so! Well, I am so glad Betsy found her. We'll take her right over. What did you say her name is?"

When Mother hung up the receiver, she said, "Well, what do you think, Betsy! She belongs to Mrs. Jackson's new maid and her name is Lillybell. They moved into the apartment over the garage this morning. Lillybell wandered off while they were busy with the moving van. Her mother has been looking everywhere for her. Mrs. Jackson telephoned the police an hour ago."

Betsy put Lillybell down and slid out of the chair. "Oh, Mother," she cried, "then Lillybell is going to live right on the other side of the garden wall, too?"

"That's right," said Mother.

"Then I can play with her, just as though she was 'dopted, can't I?" said Betsy.

"Of course you can," replied Mother.

Mother and Betsy each took hold of one of Lillybell's little hands. Lillybell's lollipop was all gone now. They walked around to the Jacksons' house. Lillybell's mother and Mrs. Jackson were at the front gate when they arrived.

The colored woman ran toward them and picked up Lillybell. The tears were running down her face. "Oh, Lillybell!" she cried. "My little Lillybell! What fo' you go 'way from yo' Mammy?"

Lillybell patted her mother's cheek and said, in a very tiny voice, "Mammy!"

"Mother," cried Betsy, "Lillybell can talk. She just said 'Mammy'!"

Lillybell's mother thanked Betsy and her mother for bringing Lillybell back to her.

"I'm glad I found her," said Betsy. "If she hadn't had any mother or father, we would have 'dopted her . . . maybe."

CHAPTER X

THE EASTER CHICK

AT EASTER TIME Billy brought a little chick to school. It was a round fuzzy ball of cream-color fluff. He brought it in a box with holes poked in the lid. The little chick said "Peep, peep, peep" all the way to school.

Miss Ross was never surprised at anything Billy brought to school and so she wasn't surprised at the Easter chick.

"She's for you, Miss Ross," said Billy. "Her name is Daisy."

"Thank you very much, Billy," said Miss Ross. "I am afraid I won't have any place to keep her in my apartment, so I guess we will have to keep her here at school. You will all have to help me raise Daisy."

The children were delighted to know that they were going to have a little chicken to raise. Billy was as pleased as could be, for he had been very fond of the chick ever since he had first laid eyes on it.

"Where will we keep it?" asked Betsy.

"You children will have to make a place in which to keep it," said Miss Ross. "What kind of place will the little chicken need?"

"I know," said Peter, raising his hand.

"Well, you tell us, Peter," said Miss Ross.

"It will need a little wooden house with a roost in it and a nice box for a nest," said Peter.

"I know something else it will need," said Betsy.

"And what is that?" asked Miss Ross.

"It will need a place to run where it can scratch up little worms and bugs and gravel," said Betsy.

"Peep, peep, peep," came from the box.

"That's right," said Miss Ross. "So where will we have to build the house for the chicken?"

"Outside," said Ellen.

"Then we will have to get some chicken wire," said Kenny, "so that it won't get lost."

"Yes," said Miss Ross. "Can anyone think of anything else that we will need?"

The children sat thinking for a moment. Then Christopher's face lit up. "I know," he said; "some straw for the nest."

"Yes," said Miss Ross, "straw for the nest."

"How soon will she begin to lay eggs?" asked Sally.

"Oh, not for quite some time," said Miss Ross. "Probably not for several months."

"Oh, Miss Ross," said Betsy, "maybe our class could sell the eggs and make some money for the school fund."

"Maybe so," said Miss Ross.

"Peep, peep, peep," said Daisy.

"But some day Daisy will have little chickens and they will lay a lot of eggs," said Ellen.

"We have some empty cardboard boxes for eggs at home," said Mary Lou. "I can bring them to put the eggs in."

"Now before you begin to prepare for the eggs," said Miss Ross, "let's get Daisy's house built."

"Her house and her yard," said Billy.

"Peep, peep, peep," went the chick.

"She will have to have a bigger box right away," said Miss Ross. "I'm afraid she isn't very happy in this small one."

"Maybe we can get one from Mr. Windrim," said Kenny.

"You and Billy can go see," said Miss Ross.

Kenny and Billy started off to find Mr. Windrim. Soon they returned with a wooden box about two feet long and a foot wide. It wasn't very deep but the sides of the box were a little higher than the chick.

"Oh, that is very nice," said Miss Ross.

Billy put the chick in the box and sprinkled some gravel over the bottom.

"What are we going to feed Daisy?" asked Peter.

"She ought to have some food."

"Peep, peep, peep," said Daisy.

"Oh, I forgot," cried Billy. "I brought some corn meal to school."

Billy went to the cloak-room and brought out a little bag of corn meal. He put some in a dish and moistened it with water. Then he put the dish in the box. He also put a dish of water in. The box was placed in a corner of the room.

Daisy seemed happier now. She didn't peep quite so often and the children went on with the day's work.

The next morning the children in the third grade came to school loaded down.

Kenny came in with a large wooden box. "Look what I brought to make a house for Daisy," said Kenny. "Isn't it a dandy?"

In a few moments Peter came in with a great big box. "Won't this make a fine house for Daisy?" he said.

Right behind him was Teddy. He, too, had a big box. "This is for a house for Daisy," he said.

"Goodness!" said Miss Ross, as two more boys came

in with boxes. "Daisy will have a whole apartment house to live in if we use all of those boxes."

When the twins arrived they had their express wagon with them. In the express wagon was a big roll of chicken wire. "Here's the chicken wire," they said. "Our daddy had it in the cellar."

When Betsy arrived she was carrying a big paper bag filled with straw. "This is for Daisy's nest," she said.

Mary Lou came in with a pile of empty egg boxes. They were piled up so high she could hardly see over them.

"Gracious me!" cried Miss Ross. "Daisy will be kept very busy if she has to fill all of those boxes."

Then Christopher appeared, dragging a sack of cracked corn. "I got it from the feed store," said Christopher. "I told the man who keeps the store that we were going to raise chickens at our school and he gave me all this. It was so heavy I grew tired of carrying it."

By nine o'clock the whole front of the room was

filled with things for Daisy. No baby chick ever had more things than Daisy. About the only thing the children hadn't brought were the worms and bugs.

Everyone was so much interested in all of the things that had been brought for Daisy that no one thought to look for her until after the bell rang. Then Billy went to her box to give her some fresh water. What did he find but an empty box! There was no little chick.

"Daisy's gone!" cried Billy. "She isn't here."

"Not there!" said Miss Ross.

All of the children crowded around the box. Daisy was certainly not there.

"Well, she must be in the room somewhere," said Miss Ross.

The children began to search the room. They looked in the corners and under Miss Ross's desk, but there was no little chick. They looked in the cloak-room and even in the wastepaper basket. The chick could not be found.

They searched everywhere. Finally Miss Ross said they would have to get on with their day's work.

"She will turn up by-and-by," said Miss Ross. "She can't be very far away."

The children tried hard to keep their minds on spelling and reading and numbers, but they kept thinking about Daisy.

"Daisy peeped all day yesterday," said Billy, "and now she won't peep at all. It's just as though she hid on purpose."

In the middle of the morning some petals dropped from some flowers on Miss Ross's desk. Betsy went to the back of the room and got the dust pan and brush. The dust pan was one that was partly covered by a little tin roof. Betsy put the pan down on the floor. Just as she was about to sweep up the petals out walked the little round ball of a chick.

"Here's Daisy!" cried Betsy.

The children laughed when they saw Daisy. They were so glad to find her. Betsy picked her up and put her back in the box.

The boys covered the box with wire screening so that Daisy wouldn't get lost again.

The best wooden box was selected for Daisy's house. Then the children spent several weeks building her house and yard. They put it out of doors, near the school garden. The spot was shaded by some trees and the earth seemed rich.

"There ought to be plenty of worms and bugs in that earth," said Billy.

By the time the new quarters were finished Daisy had grown big enough to be kept out of doors.

Each week a different group of children took care of feeding her. The group was known as "The Daisy Committee."

Daisy was growing into a very beautiful chicken. She was pure white. The children could hardly wait for her to lay her first egg. The pile of empty boxes on the table in the classroom grew higher and higher.

Every day the children looked in the nest to see if Daisy had laid an egg. But the nest was always empty.

One day Peter came to school with a china egg. "It's for Daisy," he said. "I got thinking that maybe Daisy doesn't know that she's supposed to lay eggs. Maybe if

we show her this, it will put her in mind of it."

The china egg was laid in Daisy's nest. Daisy paid no attention to it.

One day Betsy and Billy looked in the nest. There lay the china egg all alone.

"If she doesn't begin to lay eggs soon," said Billy, "school will be over."

Suddenly Daisy stretched her neck. She seemed to swell up and her feathers stood out. The children stared at her. Billy grabbed hold of Betsy. "She's going to lay one now," he gasped.

"It will break," said Betsy. "She's supposed to be on her nest."

Like a flash Billy picked up the chicken and carried her to her nest. Billy patted the nest with his hand. "You lay 'em there," he said to Daisy.

Daisy didn't look one bit interested. Billy tried to push her down on the nest but she struggled and got free. In a moment she was back in her yard.

Again she stretched her neck and swelled her body. Suddenly she let out a noise that sounded like "Cock-a-doodle-doo!"

Betsy's eyes popped. She looked at Billy. "I never heard a hen make a noise like that," she said.

"They make noises when they lay eggs," said Billy. "Maybe she's just practicing."

Once again Daisy stretched her neck. This time it was loud and long. "Cock-a-doodle-doo! Cock-a-doodle-doo!"

"Billy," said Betsy, "Daisy's just been fooling us all the time. She's not a hen at all. She's a rooster. And she's not a she; she's a he. And roosters don't lay eggs."

Betsy and Billy ran back to their classroom. They were so excited they could hardly speak. "Daisy's a rooster!" gasped Billy.

"She's crowing," said Betsy. "I mean, he's crowing."

The children could hear Daisy crowing now. He seemed to be crowing his head off.

"Listen to her," said Billy. "I mean, listen to him."

The children were so provoked at Daisy for turning out to be a rooster that they hardly went near him for days. They felt that he had purposely cheated them out of all of the money they had expected to make from the eggs.

Finally Peter said, "I think we should change Daisy's name. Who ever heard of a boy named Daisy?"

"Guess we better name him Big Ben," said Richard. "He certainly goes off like an alarm clock."

So the rooster was named Big Ben.

When it came time for school to close, the children had grown very fond of Big Ben. They had forgiven him for being a rooster.

Miss Ross said that something would have to be done about him for the summer. "He can't stay here," she said, "and I can't keep him in my apartment. Billy, I guess I will have to give him back to you."

The last day of school Billy carried the rooster home. He needed a much larger box than the day he brought him to school.

At home he made a little pen for him but he was always getting out. He dug up the flower beds and made a great deal of noise.

The neighbors complained because he crowed early in the morning and woke them up.

Finally Billy's daddy said that Billy would have to get rid of Big Ben.

"What can I do with him?" asked Billy, in a troubled voice.

"Well, all that he is good for is stewing," said Billy's daddy.

"Oh, Daddy! We can't stew Big Ben," cried Billy.

"Something will have to be done about him," said Daddy. "So you had better think hard and fast."

Billy talked it all over with Betsy. Then Betsy had an idea. "I know what!" she cried. "You can send him up to Grandaddy on the farm. He has hundreds of chickens and he would be glad to have Big Ben."

Billy thought this was a good idea. He set to work at once making a crate for Big Ben. When it was finished, he put the rooster in and nailed slats across so that he couldn't get out. His daddy painted the name and address on the crate. Then Betsy and Billy and his daddy took it to the station. There they put it on the train.

There were tears in Billy's and Betsy's eyes when they saw the rooster go.

The next week, Betsy received a letter from Grandaddy. This is what the letter said:

"DEAR BETSY,

Big Ben arrived safely and I have written to Billy to thank him for sending me such a fine rooster. I told

Billy that Big Ben seems a little homesick, so I think Billy had better come up with you and Ellen and spend the summer on the farm.

Love and kisses from

GRANDADDY."

THE END

VOYAGER BOOKS

AVB 1 Karin Anckarsvärd
THE MYSTERIOUS SCHOOLMASTER

AVB 2 Margot Benary-Isbert
BLUE MYSTERY

AVB 3 Roger Burlingame
INVENTORS BEHIND THE INVENTOR

AVB 4 Elizabeth K. Cooper
SCIENCE IN YOUR OWN BACK YARD

AVB 5 Edward Eager
KNIGHT'S CASTLE

AVB 6 Eleanor Estes
THE WITCH FAMILY

AVB 7 C. H. Frick
THE COMEBACK GUY

AVB 8 Carolyn Haywood
HERE'S A PENNY

AVB 9 Dorothy Lyons
DARK SUNSHINE

AVB 11 Mary Norton
THE BORROWERS

AVB 12 Carl Sandburg
WIND SONG

AVB 14 Virginia Sorensen
PLAIN GIRL

AVB 15 William O. Steele
THE PERILOUS ROAD

AVB 16 Yoshiko Uchida
THE MAGIC LISTENING CAP

AVB 17 Nina Brown Baker
NICKELS AND DIMES

AVB 18 George Barrow
YOUR WORLD IN MOTION

AVB 19 L. M. Boston
THE RIVER AT GREEN KNOWE

AVB 20 Marjorie Braymer
THE WALLS OF WINDY TROY

AVB 21 Madye Lee Chastain
EMMY KEEPS A PROMISE

AVB 22 Helen F. Daringer
STEPSISTER SALLY

AVB 23 Elizabeth Enright
GONE-AWAY LAKE

AVB 24 László Hámori
DANGEROUS JOURNEY

AVB 26 Ivan Kušan
THE MYSTERY OF GREEN HILL

AVB 27 Mildred Lawrence
PEACHTREE ISLAND

AVB 28 C. J. Maginley
HISTORIC MODELS OF EARLY AMERICA

AVB 29 Helen Rushmore
COWBOY JOE OF THE CIRCLE S

AVB 30 E. C. Spykman
TERRIBLE, HORRIBLE EDIE

AVB 31 Alfred Stefferud
THE WONDERS OF SEEDS

AVB 32 Henry Winterfeld
DETECTIVES IN TOGAS

AVB 33 Julie F. Batchelor and Claudia de Lys
SUPERSTITIOUS? HERE'S WHY!

AVB 34 Michel-Aimé Baudouy
MORE THAN COURAGE

AVB 35 Lorraine Beim
TRIUMPH CLEAR

AVB 36 Margot Benary-Isbert
THE ARK

AVB 37 Andrée Clair
BEMBA: An African Adventure

AVB 38 Elizabeth K. Cooper
SCIENCE ON THE SHORES AND BANKS

AVB 39 A. J. Dawson
FINN THE WOLFHOUND

AVB 40 Jeanette Eaton
LONE JOURNEY

AVB 41 Anne Guthrie
MADAME AMBASSADOR

AVB 42 Leif Hamre
LEAP INTO DANGER

AVB 43 Carol Kendall
THE GAMMAGE CUP

AVB 44 Stephen W. Meader
WHO RIDES IN THE DARK?

AVB 45 Joan Phipson
THE FAMILY CONSPIRACY

AVB 46 Kathrene Pinkerton
HIDDEN HARBOR

AVB 47 Sigurd Senje
ESCAPE!

AVB 48 Miriam Young
THE SECRET OF STONE HOUSE FARM

AVB 49 Karin Anckarsvärd
THE ROBBER GHOST

AVB 50 Eleanor Estes
THE MOFFATS

AVB 51 Carolyn Haywood
"B" IS FOR BETSY

AVB 52 Eleanor F. Lattimore
LITTLE PEAR

AVB 53 Dorothy Lyons
BLUE SMOKE

AVB 54 Stephen W. Meader
SPARKPLUG OF THE HORNETS

AVB 55 Andre Norton
STAND TO HORSE

AVB 56 William O. Steele
THE BUFFALO KNIFE

AVB 57 Karin Anckarsvärd
MADCAP MYSTERY

AVB 58 Harold Courlander
THE KING'S DRUM

AVB 59 Edward Eager
HALF MAGIC

AVB 60 Mary Norton
THE BORROWERS AFIELD

AVB 61 E. C. Spykman
EDIE ON THE WARPATH

AVB 62 Jacqueline Ayer
NU DANG AND HIS KITE

AVB 63 Marcia Brown
THE THREE BILLY GOATS GRUFF

AVB 64 Alice Vaught Davis
TIMOTHY TURTLE

AVB 65 Eleanor Estes
GINGER PYE

AVB 66 James Flora
MY FRIEND CHARLIE

AVB 67 Antonio Frasconi
SEE AND SAY: A Picture Book in Four Languages

AVB 68 John Langstaff and Feodor Rojankovsky
FROG WENT A-COURTIN'

AVB 69 Virginia Sorensen
MIRACLES ON MAPLE HILL

AVB 70 William O. Steele
FLAMING ARROWS

AVB 71 P. L. Travers
MARY POPPINS

AVB 72 Helen F. Daringer
ADOPTED JANE

AVB 73 Fritz Eichenberg
APE IN A CAPE: An Alphabet of Odd Animals

AVB 74 Elizabeth Enright
RETURN TO GONE-AWAY

AVB 75 Brothers Grimm and Harriet Pincus
LITTLE RED RIDING HOOD

AVB 76 Carolyn Haywood
BACK TO SCHOOL WITH BETSY

AVB 77 John Langstaff and Feodor Rojankovsky
OVER IN THE MEADOW

AVB 78 Mary Norton
THE BORROWERS AFLOAT

AVB 79 Ann and Paul Rand
I KNOW A LOT OF THINGS

AVB 80 James Thurber
MANY MOONS

AVB 81 Will and Nicolas
FINDERS KEEPERS